DEMONS IN THE DARKNESS 2

LessonsForLifeBooks.com

IMPRINT A Cross Man Comics Adventure

Demons in the
Darkness 2

© 2016 by
Keith M. Hammond
is published by
Lessons for Life Books, Inc.
St. Paul, MN 55116

ISBN 13: 978-1938588976. Printed in the U.S.A.

Cover design and layout by Keith M. Hammond.
Story concept and 3D Illustrations by Keith M. Hammond.
NOTE: Several software applications and 3D models and 3D props were used to create and generate and render the scenes and characters contained within this and other Cross Man Comics adventures. All are used by purchase or permission.

CROSSMAN
BOOKS

CIRCUIT...
I can't just leave
in the middle
OF A BATTLE !!!

6

Like the first one... this new building also came out of nowhere.

When the blaze bomb exploded in that lava lake underground, it moved several layers of earth and this is what rose to the surface.

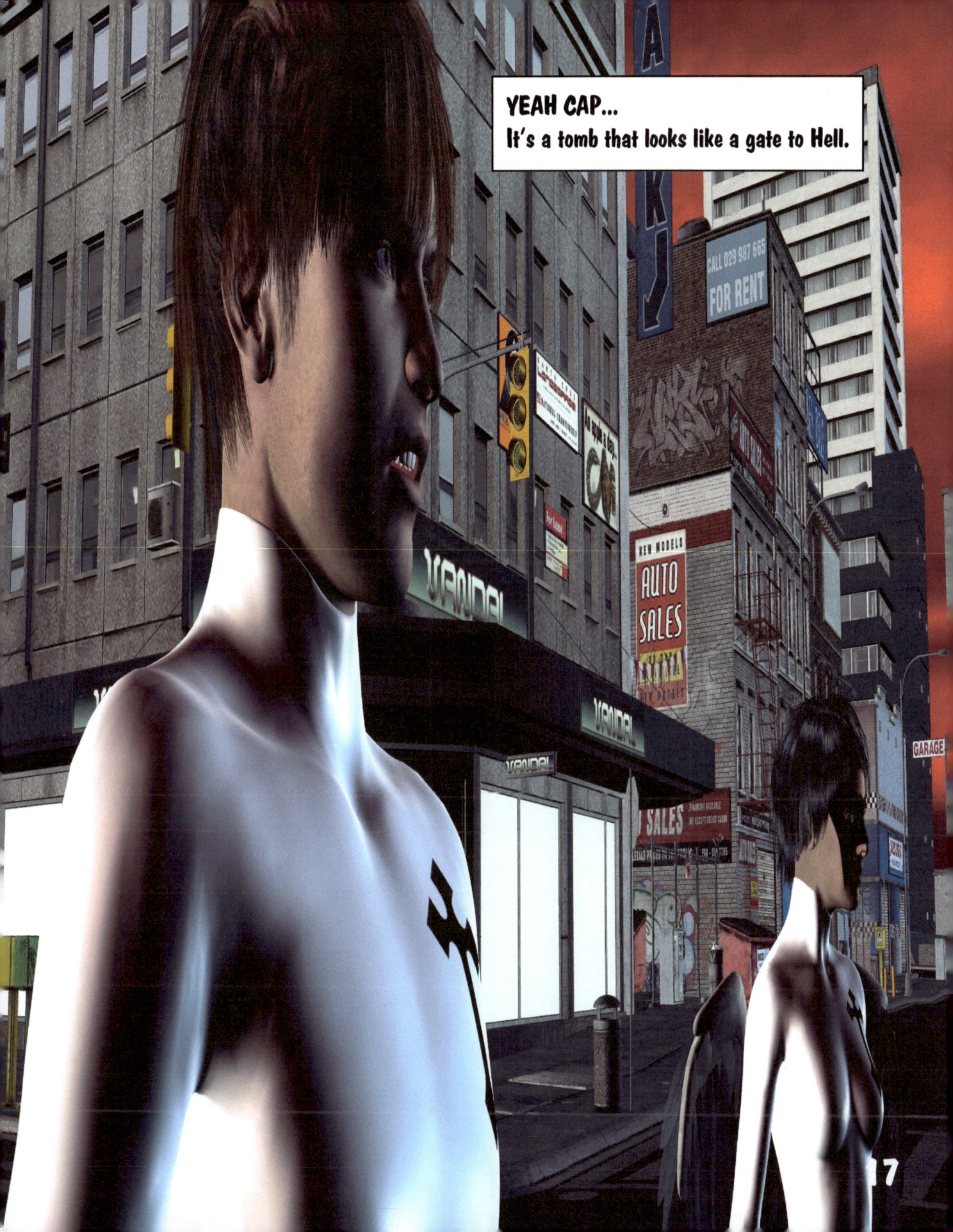

CAP, people are coming from miles around just to walk in....and sign away their soul.

They're all walking up willingly.

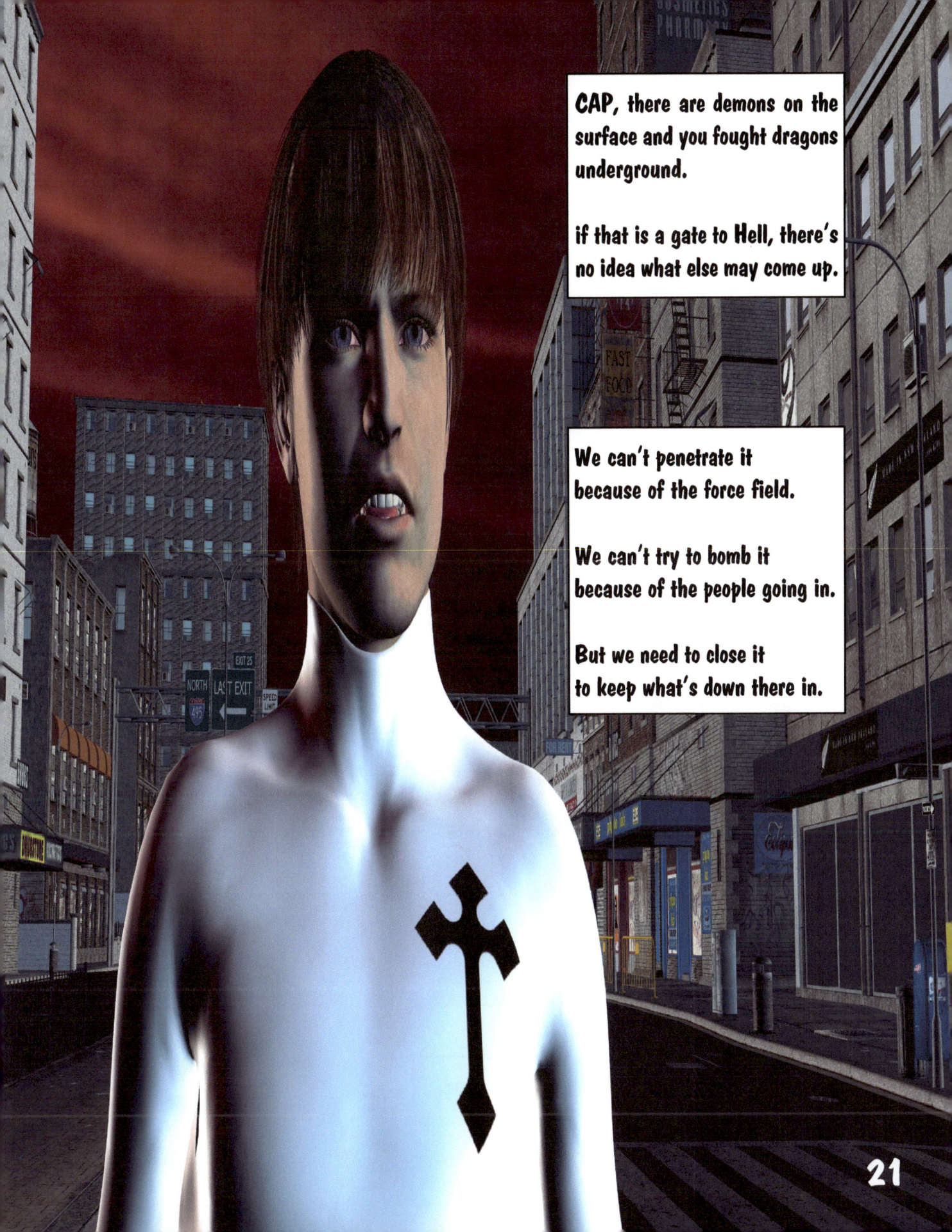

CAP, there are demons on the surface and you fought dragons underground.

if that is a gate to Hell, there's no idea what else may come up.

We can't penetrate it because of the force field.

We can't try to bomb it because of the people going in.

But we need to close it to keep what's down there in.

RANGER...
Find a weak spot in that force field or a way to reverse the polarity.

RIGHT AWAY SIR!!!

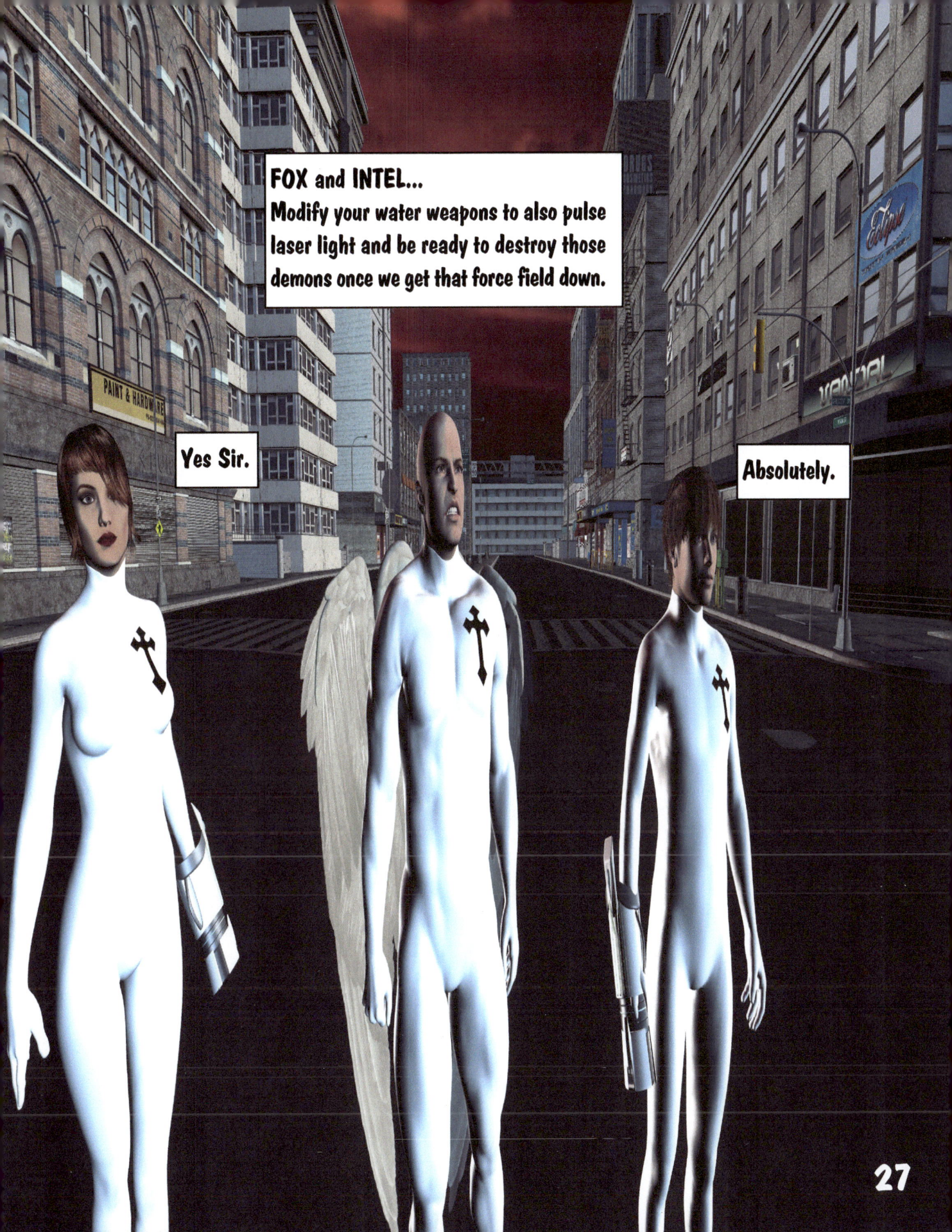

CAP, this is **CIRCUIT**,
There may be a way into the tomb, but you have to access it from the dungeon you just left. There's an old tunnel inside a lava lake that stretches from the tomb over to that old church...but all our sensors show some much bigger demons and dragons down there.

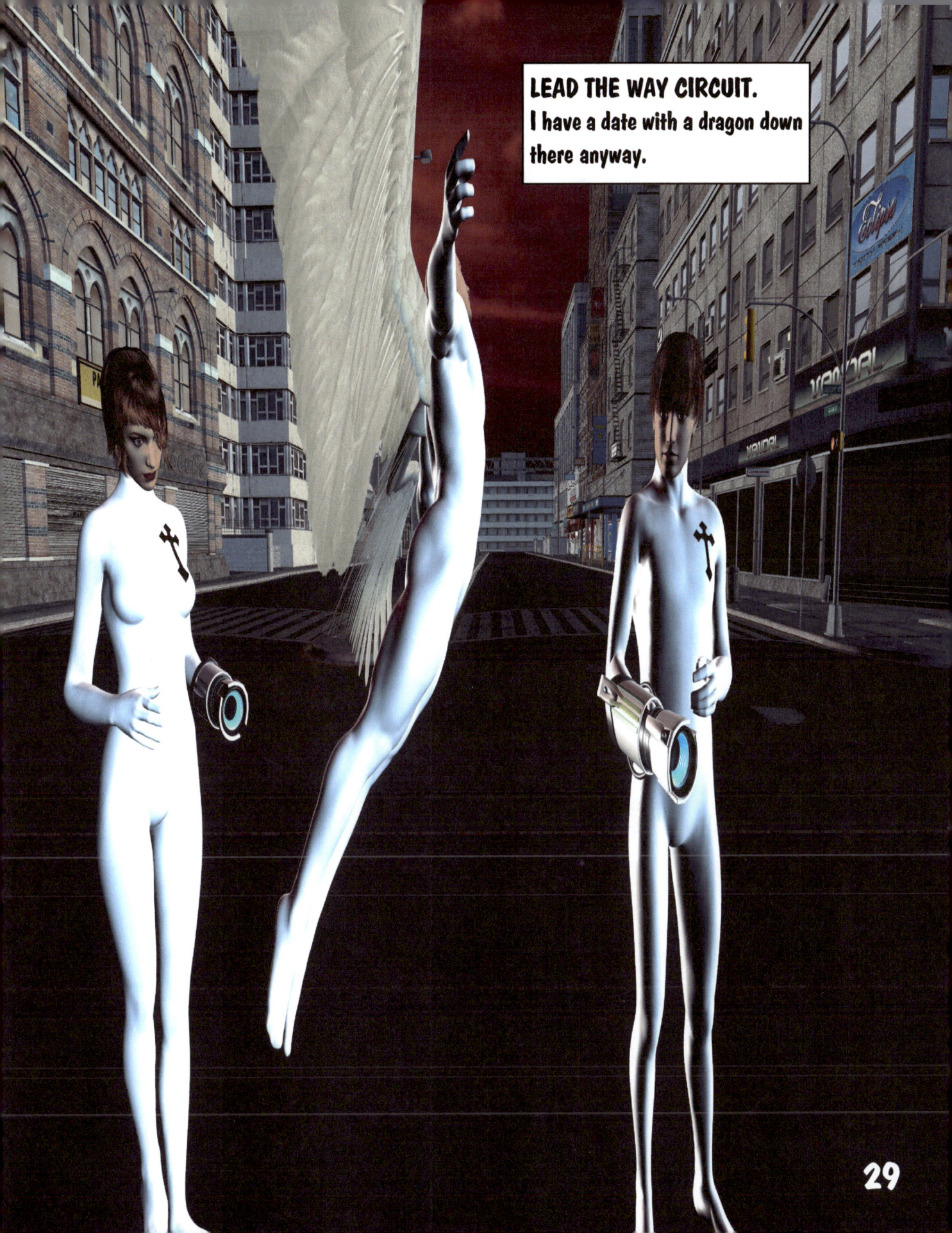

When **CAP** makes it back to the dungeon...the dragon is waiting.

His anger over seeing people signing away their souls...propels him forward.

He wastes no time thrusting his bayonet into the belly of the beast.

31

A hit to the heart of the dragon does damage,

but CAP wants to be sure the damage is deadly.

33

A vital vein brings victory.

DRAGON,
when you get down there,
tell your boss I'm on my way
to find him.

TEAM, this dragon is dead. I'm going through a door to go much deeper into this dark and demonic dungeon.

I have to search for Satan.

Give me a status report...

CAP, it's SHADOW...
I've created a mirror in front of the entrance.
When people look into it, seeing their own
reflection is stopping them in their tracks.

It seems to awaken them from their zombie-
like state. I'll keep this up as long as I can.

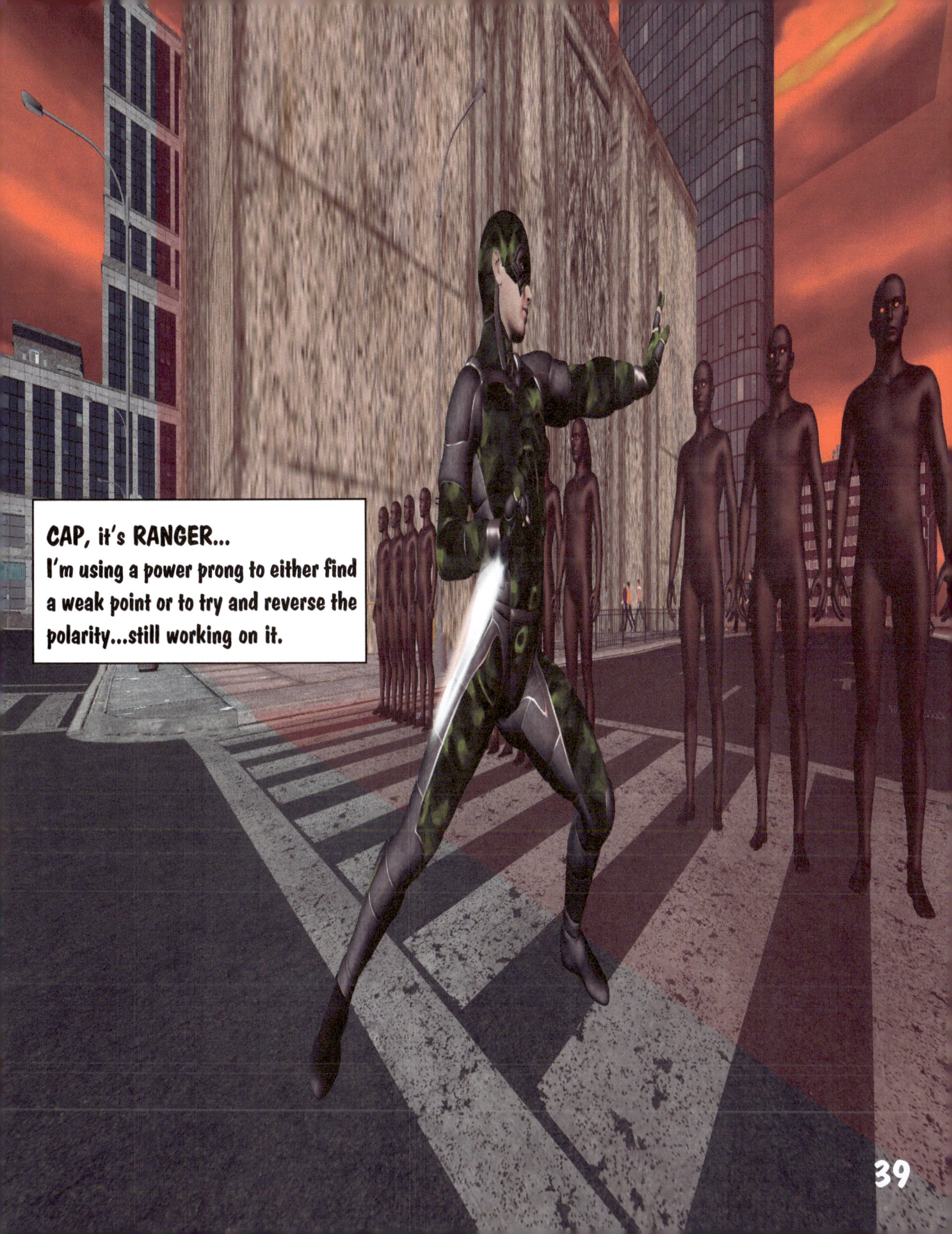

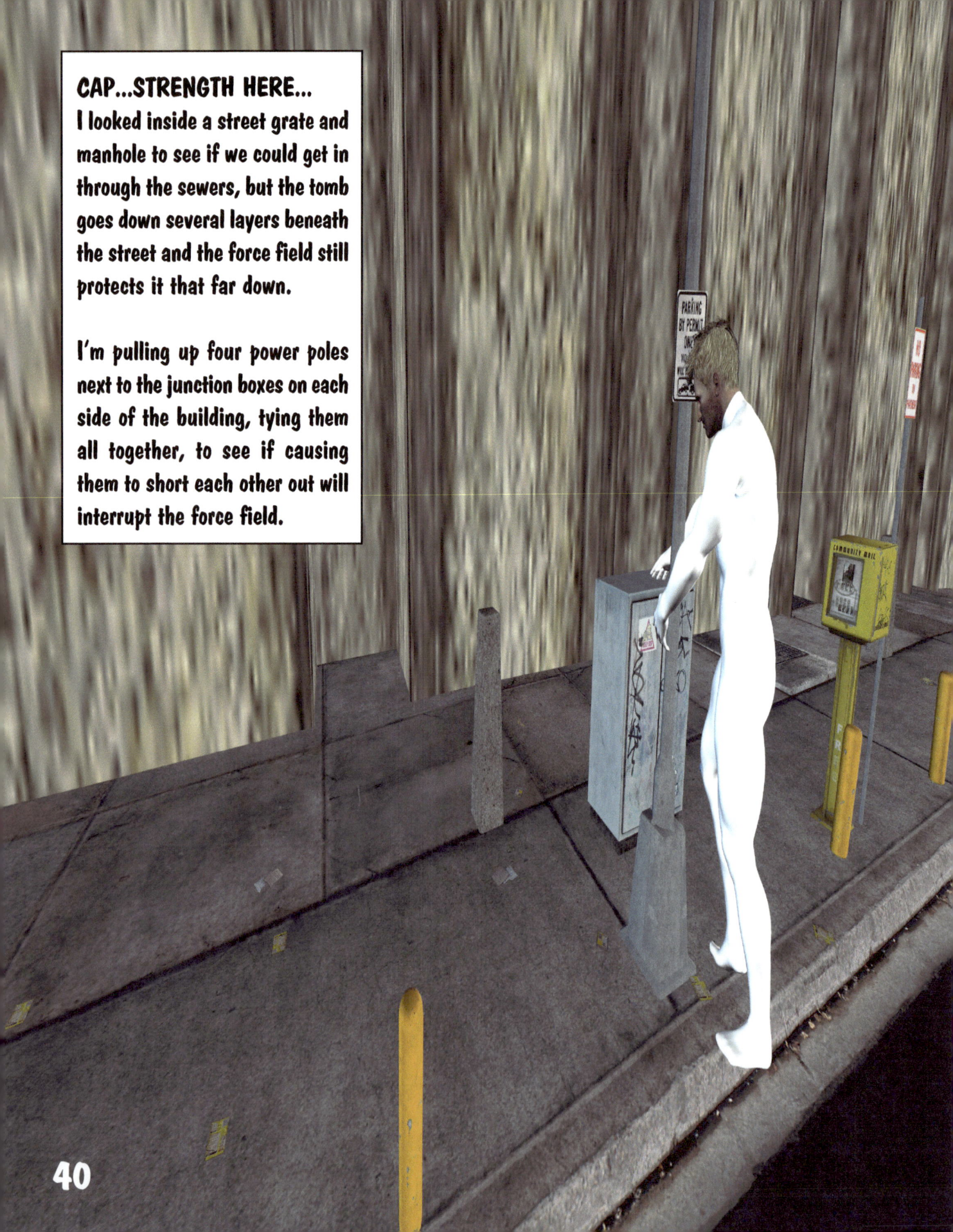

CAP...STRENGTH HERE...
I looked inside a street grate and manhole to see if we could get in through the sewers, but the tomb goes down several layers beneath the street and the force field still protects it that far down.

I'm pulling up four power poles next to the junction boxes on each side of the building, tying them all together, to see if causing them to short each other out will interrupt the force field.

SOUNDS GOOD...
KEEP ME POSTED.
I've made it to the lava lake.

There's a tunnel built into the
walls. I'm going through another
door. CAP OUT.

Before **CAP** reaches the door...
he sees another adversary.

AHHH...
You must be looking for your fanged
friend I tossed in the lava.

44

More than happy to send you there with him.

Let me help you get rid of that nasty growl.

How about a treat?
Here's a DEAD BAT.

When you reach out to eat it,
I'm going to kill you,
GOT IT?!

TEAM,
Listen up...

Dangerous dog down.
I'm headed into the
depths of this demonic
dungeon...

I'm going to search for
Satan and put an end
to this...once and for all.

Prepare yourselves to join the battle down here.

See more of this
amazing adventure
in **PART THREE**
of the next issue of
Cross Man,
Demons in the Darkness!